Samuel French Acting Edition

The Way of the World

by Theresa Rebeck

FOR PRODUCTION ENQUIRIES

UNITED STATES AND CANADA
Info@SamuelFrench.com
1-866-598-8449

UNITED KINGDOM AND EUROPE
Plays@SamuelFrench.co.uk
020-7255-4302

Each title is subject to availability from Samuel French, depending upon country of performance. Please be aware that *THE WAY OF THE WORLD* may not be licensed by Samuel French in your territory. Professional and amateur producers should contact the nearest Samuel French office or licensing partner to verify availability.

MUSIC USE NOTE

Licensees are solely responsible for obtaining formal written permission from copyright owners to use copyrighted music in the performance of this play and are strongly cautioned to do so. If no such permission is obtained by the licensee, then the licensee must use only original music that the licensee owns and controls. Licensees are solely responsible and liable for all music clearances and shall indemnify the copyright owners of the play(s) and their licensing agent, Samuel French, against any costs, expenses, losses and liabilities arising from the use of music by licensees. Please contact the appropriate music licensing authority in your territory for the rights to any incidental music.

IMPORTANT BILLING AND CREDIT REQUIREMENTS

If you have obtained performance rights to this title, please refer to your licensing agreement for important billing and credit requirements.

THE WAY OF THE WORLD opened at the Dorset Theatre Festival in Dorset, Vermont on July 28, 2016. The performance was directed by Theresa Rebeck, with set design by Narelle Sissons, lighting design by Michael Giannitti, costume design by Barbara Bell, and sound design by M.L. Dogg. The dramaturg was Margarett Perry. The cast was as follows:

CHARLES	David Turner
REG	Brian Dykstra
KATRINA	Nilanjana Bose
RENE	Kristine Nielsen
MAE	Elizabeth Evans
LYLE	Brent Langdon
WAITRESS	Katie Paxton
TOPHER	Josiah Bania

THE WAY OF THE WORLD opened at the Folger Theatre in Washington, D.C. on January 16, 2018. The performance was directed by Theresa Rebeck, with scenic design by Alexander Dodge, lighting design by Donald Holder, costume design by Linda Cho, and sound design by M.L. Dogg. The dramaturg was Michele Osherow, and the production stage manager was Carolynn Richer. The cast was as follows:

CHARLES	Brandon Espinoza
REG	Elan Zafir
KATRINA	Erica Dorfler
RENE	Kristine Nielsen
MAE	Eliza Huberth
LYLE	Daniel Morgan Shelley
WAITRESS	Ashley Austin Morris
HENRY	Luigi Sottile

CHARACTERS

CHARLES

HENRY

REG

KATRINA

RENE

MAE

LYLE

WAITRESS

ACT ONE

Scene One

(An outdoor table at a swank restaurant. A glorious sky. **HENRY** *and* **CHARLES** *are having martinis.)*

CHARLES. I hate the Hamptons. Every summer, everybody races out here to avoid all the people who are racing out here. I swear if I see one more teenage girl with a Gucci bag I'm going to commit seppuku. On her.

HENRY. I don't mind it.

CHARLES. You loathe it.

HENRY. I enjoy it. The parties are fun. The clothes. The restaurants.

CHARLES. The money. Oh wait – you don't have money.

HENRY. I have money.

CHARLES. You had money. Oh wait. You almost had money. And then –

HENRY. That is a gorgeous bag. Where'd you get this?

CHARLES. John Varvatos.

HENRY. It's a little heavy for the summer, isn't it?

CHARLES. Don't change the subject.

HENRY. I wasn't.

CHARLES. You slept with the aunt. You had six hundred million dollars falling onto your – "lap" is not exactly where it was falling, but it's close enough for today's audience –

HENRY. Ah ha ha.

CHARLES. And now we're back to door number one.

HENRY. Door number one?

CHARLES. Calling Dad for a loan.

HENRY. I don't need my father to give me a loan. I have his credit card.

(He laughs.)

CHARLES. You're still changing the subject.

HENRY. I'm sitting here having a cocktail, Charles, and admiring your bag, and thinking about getting one myself, even though it seems a bit dark for summer. Somewhat like you.

CHARLES. It's your black heart which is a bit dark.

HENRY. My heart – is hopeful.

CHARLES. It can hope all it wants, but Mae Johnson won't speak to you. Ever again. Neither will her money. Everyone east of Oyster Bay is talking about it.

HENRY. Oh god. Gossip is so boring.

CHARLES. Even when it's about you?

HENRY. Oh that's right, it's about me! Okay carry on.

(REG *and* **LYLE** *enter.* **REG** *sees* **HENRY** *and* **CHARLES,** *waves.)*

REG. Hey asshole!

(REG *and* **LYLE** *join them.)*

HENRY.	CHARLES.
Hey, Reg	Reg.

REG. You are unbelievable. You animal. You animal. You kill me you lunatic. Did you have sex with Mae Johnson's aunt?

HENRY. Yes.

REG. You're a psychopath. It's hilarious. She's like eighty years old. Did you do her?

HENRY. I –

REG. *(Looking around.)* Can I get a drink over here? Don't try to deny it. It's already legendary. You're a legend you nut. Anybody want a refill?

(To passing **WAITRESS**.*)* Just bring another round of whatever it is these hopeless losers are drinking.

(The **WAITRESS** *ignores him.)*

Did she ignore me? Seriously, did that waitress give me the brush-off?

CHARLES. Welcome to summer.

REG. Come on, it's great here. Blue skies. You can take the boat out every day. Expensive liquor. Girls in pretty dresses and hot shoes, what's not to like. Anybody want a burger?

CHARLES. They don't sell burgers here.

REG. I'm starving what do they have? I need a menu. I need some meat.

CHARLES. They do a lovely charcuterie.

REG. You're so gay, Charles.

CHARLES. And you're a throwback.

REG. I don't need a menu, I need some meat. Any kind of steak. I'll get one for you too, Henry. Raw. You animal.

(He beats himself on the chest.)

Yeah! It's summer! Where's that waitress?

*(**KATRINA** enters carrying a couple of shopping bags.)*

KATRINA. I just had lunch with Mae! She's really upset. She can't even talk about it. You so screwed this up, Henry, you're a terrible person and you deserve everything you get.

REG. Why is it terrible? He had sex with her aunt. It's weird but it's not terrible.

(Laughing.)

He had sex with Rene Johnson. She's like eighty.

KATRINA. She's not eighty! She's sixty.

HENRY. She's not sixty.

CHARLES. She's fifty-two.

REG. Same thing. Fifty-two. Eighty.

KATRINA. Stop it, it is not the same thing! Every one of you, you are all terrible men.

HENRY. What's so terrible about what I did? It made her really happy.

(All groan.)

KATRINA. Then you're not interested in Mae anymore.

HENRY. Did I say that?

CHARLES. Then you ARE interested in Mae anymore.

HENRY. Did I say I wasn't?

REG. Interested. That's a good word. That kind of money, I'm interested too.

KATRINA. What? Hey.

REG. Oh no no no no. Come on, it was a joke.

(He tries to kiss her. She shoves him.)

Come on...

(They kiss. The guys all moan.)

HENRY. Are you going to tell me what she said?

KATRINA. I asked her about it, her response was she wants to give all her money away to Haitian refugees.

(They all moan at that one.)

REG. That's bad.

HENRY. She said –

KATRINA. Yes! She wants to give all her money to the poor now.

HENRY. This is a huge misunderstanding.

KATRINA. It's not a misunderstanding! Everyone knows that Rene has been keeping Mae under lock and key because not one of you clowns can be trusted around all that money. Especially not you, Henry.

HENRY. I'm trustworthy!

KATRINA. Oh yes we're so aware. We all assumed you were just flirting with Rene so she'd let you hang around. That's what I assumed –

CHARLES. It's what everyone assumed.

KATRINA. No one assumed you'd actually – you know –

REG. Do her.

HENRY. What do you want me to say? I was drunk. It didn't seem like such a bad idea at the time. She's not unattractive and it's the sort of thing one does now, isn't it, to be polite?

REG. *(Overlap.)* Whoa.

KATRINA. *(Overlap.)* Polite? Did he just say polite?

CHARLES. *(Overlap.)* He said polite.

REG. It makes everyone really uncomfortable when you say things like that.

HENRY. There was really no way out of it at the time.
I honestly thought it was the best solution to an increasingly problematic situation.

REG. What are you SAYING?

KATRINA. Polite. You're hilarious. I'm telling you, Henry, you're toast.

(She looks at **HENRY**. *He thinks about this.)*

Scene Two

(Rene's boudoir. **RENE** *is showing off her new clothes to* **MAE.***)*

RENE. The mauve is maybe a little severe but I think the silhouette is terrific. They just got it in this afternoon and Camilla called me, she said you simply have to get down here right away, you're going to love so many of these new pieces and you know she really doesn't take the time unless she's serious. I mean, she knows that it is pointless to drag anyone down there unless she has something that is absolutely – do you think the mauve is too much? It doesn't do wonders but it's not brittle, so many colors this season are really. I don't know. I don't know, I loved the feel of it in the store but now it seems like something old ladies wear. And the color looks like you're hiding things. I don't like it. It's not, I don't –

MAE. It's nice!

RENE. Nice. Oh my god. Put a stake in my heart, nice –

MAE. Lovely –

RENE. Lovely is worse. It's not lovely. I'm fat, I look so fat in everything.

MAE. You don't –

RENE. I'm sorry. A momentary collapse into insecurity! I do love it. It's clean. It's effortlessly classic. It's chic.

MAE. Yes.

RENE. It's hideous getting old.

MAE. You're not old!

RENE. I didn't say I was old. I said I'm getting old.

MAE. We're all getting old. It's the Hamptons. I hate what I'm wearing too. These clothes out here are stupid. Why do people out here dress like this?

RENE. You look adorable. That ensemble is timeless.

MAE. Timeless is stupid, Aunt Rene. Timeless is dead, if you think about it. What's timeless? Rocks. Planets.

Chanel pumps, which don't look good on anybody. You know what, we should go somewhere else. Can we go somewhere else?

RENE. You're upset.

MAE. Yes I am upset because I don't like the Hamptons. It's too hot. We all leave New York because it gets too hot in the summer and then we come to the beach, where it's even hotter. And the people are the same people! Well that's stating the obvious. But seriously if you can't get away from the weather don't you think you'd at least be able to get away from the people?

RENE. Oh I know! We could go to Paris, and stay in your mother's apartment.

MAE. Mom's not in her apartment? Where is she?

RENE. You remember. She was going to Japan for the summer.

MAE. Why?

RENE. I don't remember.

MAE. Is she still coming here for a week?

RENE. Darling you know she loves you. It breaks her heart that she can't be with you. When you were little, every time she made plans it was so painful, I was there, it was very hard for her to push the reservation confirmed button, because she was so sad about leaving you.

MAE. We don't need to talk about Mom, Aunt Rene.

RENE. And those times neither one of us could be there and we had to leave you with the maid. It was horrible. Really, darling, I think both of us are still carrying a lot of guilt about it.

MAE. Well, don't. I had a great time with Consuela. She was a lot of fun. We used to watch Zorro together, "Zorro is for the people!" It was the closest I got to a social education.

RENE. I'm glad you have some good memories.

MAE. I have lots of good memories, Aunt Rene. You were a terrific mother. Much better than Mom.

RENE. No no no! Don't say that! I am much too young to be your mother. I am your adoring, and young, maiden aunt. Not a maiden aunt, that sounds like spinster. I am your adoring and stylish older sister kind of aunt.

MAE. You can be whatever kind of aunt you want.

RENE. Good. You know what? I don't think it's a good idea to go to Paris.

MAE. I didn't want to go to Paris. You wanted to go to Paris. I want to go to Haiti.

RENE. Haiti?

MAE. Rich people did a lot of damage to that country. I'd like to get involved.

RENE. Get involved?

MAE. Yes, you know. Help.

RENE. Oh no, no, no. The truth is, Mae – frankly, that might look too much like running away.

MAE. Running away? I'm not running away.

RENE. I didn't say you were running away. I said it looks like it.

MAE. Why is what it looks like more important than what it is?

RENE. Because that is what people will believe. And what people believe is what they talk about. And what they talk about becomes the truth.

MAE. No it doesn't.

RENE. But people think it's the truth.

MAE. Aunt Rene, people out here don't think at all.

RENE. You are so funny.

MAE. I'm not trying to be funny.

RENE. Darling I'm really touched – completely, completely moved, honestly – that you care so much about me, and my feelings about what happened.

MAE. Well of course I care.

RENE. I'm fine. I hate him, but I'm fine.

MAE. I know you are.

RENE. Your little friend Henry is a disgusting pig and I'd love to take a pickaxe to his head!

(She laughs.)

MAE. He's not my friend.

RENE. He's not mine either. Seriously, I am fine!

MAE. Oh good.

RENE. The sex wasn't that good. He's gorgeous but that is the most you can say about him.

(She starts to tear up.)

MAE. Oh no no no –

RENE. I shouldn't have told you about it. It's so humiliating.

MAE. How is it humiliating?

RENE. I really thought he cared about me.

MAE. That makes two of us.

RENE. *(Getting it together.)* Oh listen. There are plenty of gorgeous men out there, I don't need to tell you that. I'm not giving it another thought.

MAE. We should get out of here. Seriously Aunt Rene, I don't want to be here all summer anyway. It's just – it's really awfully hot.

RENE. Absolutely not. No! We are NOT going to Paris.

MAE. Not Paris. Haiti.

RENE. *(Laughing.)* Haiti! You are so funny.

MAE. I'm not kidding, I'm not trying to be funny.

RENE. Mae, my good sweet girl. We can't go to Haiti. Talk about the heat! Also you know that country is really a mess, just a mess.

MAE. Which is why I want to take some of my money and do something with it to help! We could build a school, or a whole hospital, a water plant!

RENE. Wait wait wait. I know what will make us feel better! We'll throw a wonderful party!

(Blackout.)

Scene Three

(CHARLES and KATRINA in a restaurant, entering.)

CHARLES. Was not invited?

KATRINA. Mae and Rene Johnson are throwing the bash of the century and Henry was not invited.

(They laugh.)

CHARLES. Well done, brava.

KATRINA. I didn't do anything!

CHARLES. Oh honey please remember who you're talking to.

KATRINA. You started this one –

CHARLES. I told you that Henry and Mae were sleeping with each other and Rene had no idea.

KATRINA. You told me –

CHARLES. And then you went and told Rene all about it and the whole thing blew up, because he had also had sex with Rene the night before.

KATRINA. Yeah, you didn't tell me that part. You left that part out.

CHARLES. I didn't.

KATRINA. Don't even try it. You wanted that thing to blow up, and you didn't want your fingerprints on it.

CHARLES. You make me sound so clever.

KATRINA. It WASN'T that clever because I figured it all out as soon as it happened, you didn't exactly cover your tracks.

CHARLES. That is not what happened.

KATRINA. It is exactly what happened! Not that I care. I mean it serves him right. Henry is such a slut, he's a complete man-whore. And I thought Rene deserved to know. But the fact is you used me and I'm kind of mad at you.

CHARLES. If I had told you the whole story would that have changed things? You were the one –

KATRINA. Oh no –

CHARLES. I felt like I had given you a birthday present. You wanted that whole thing to blow up on him.

KATRINA. Why indeed.

CHARLES. You're hilarious.

KATRINA. So glad to amuse you. It's my ultimate dream.

CHARLES. You do amuse me. You want him back.

KATRINA. Henry? He's cute but he honestly is not all that. The sex just isn't that good.

CHARLES. Keep telling yourself.

KATRINA. Henry and I were over at Christmas.

CHARLES. You and Henry were over before you started.

KATRINA. You know, Charles, I know gay men think it's okay to hate women, but when you do it in front of us I think it counts as being rude.

CHARLES. Careful, your claws are showing.

KATRINA. My claws? You're practically licking yourself with delight. You're completely living in the retarded gay male fantasy that all straight men are secretly gay – oh not all, just the cute ones – and that women are pathetic for thinking that we actually have a use on this planet. Other than modeling couture for you clowns.

CHARLES. That's a fantasy? Are you sure?

KATRINA. You're ridiculous.

CHARLES. Perhaps so but let me tell you something. If it weren't for that vintage Louis Vuitton bag, I would never even speak to you. It, however, is fabulous.

(They both laugh at themselves.)

KATRINA. You gave it to me.

CHARLES. I did, because I love you.

(They kiss.)

Scene Four

(**REG, LYLE,** *and* **HENRY.**)

HENRY. They're having a party?

REG. Yeah some cocktail thing. You didn't get invited? Ouch. Half of Manhattan was invited.

HENRY. I don't need to go to any more parties. There's a party every minute out here. Everyone is so terrified of their own money they can't stop drinking! Meanwhile the money just keeps growing! Like the houses and the women's breasts. Seriously, we might as well move to Texas. I have better things to do than go to a party.

REG. Like what?

HENRY. Are you going?

REG. Shit yeah I'm going. Everybody's going.

HENRY. Are you going? Who are you, anyway?

REG. Oh! Shit, didn't I ever introduce you guys? I'm retarded. This is my cousin, Lyle. He's from Boston.

HENRY. Nice to meet you.

REG. Yeah, his family has a place on Nantucket but the ceiling fell in or something.

LYLE. Water damage.

REG. Water damage! And the whole place is a gut and he was stuck in Boston where it's fucking hot in the summer so I said you know, come here.

HENRY. You're cousins –

REG. Second cousins right?

LYLE. Once removed.

HENRY. I can't remember, what does once removed mean?

LYLE. It means no one wants to admit that we're related but what can you do, there's no place else to go in the summer.

REG. No, you know what it means, it means that your grandfather got the nice place in Nantucket and my grandmother got nothing so they let my dad use the place in Nantucket for a couple of weeks in the fall every now and then, but now the place in Nantucket the ceiling fell in –

LYLE. Water damage –

REG. WATER damage so now this clown needs a place to stay and everybody wants me to go back to Harvard and finish up my fucking MBA which is I would rather put my own eyes out and they think Lyle will be a good influence so he's living with me in my sister's place in Amagansett. So that's what "once removed" means.

HENRY. Are you a good influence?

LYLE. It's still unclear.

REG. Oh no he's fucking awesome, he's a fucking awesome roommate. He does the dishes and cleans up the bathroom, I'm like dude, you got to leave something for the maid to do or she feels like you're going to fire her. And that's shitty, to make someone worry that they might lose their job. I think it's unethical.

LYLE. He has some very advanced ideas about ethics.

REG. Fuck you, asshole.

LYLE. No.

HENRY. So no one here knows you.

REG. No no I'm introducing him to people. I'm going to take him to this party.

HENRY. If you can take him why can't you take me?

REG. I thought you didn't want to go.

HENRY. I need to talk to Mae.

REG. So text her.

HENRY. I'd rather talk to her.

REG. She won't return your texts?

HENRY. I don't text people. I talk to them.

REG. Listen Henry, she's not going to talk to you and Rene will flip and it will just be a scene. You'll just make things worse, and Mae is already really pissed.

HENRY. She's in a bad mood.

REG. Yeah she is in a bad mood, I think you could say that, yes.

LYLE. Who is this "Mae"?

REG.   **HENRY.**

  Yeah.   Yes.

LYLE. And she's?

REG. She's a liberal, which, okay I like liberals but they have no sense of humor.

HENRY. She's actually very funny.

LYLE. Is she pretty?

REG.   **HENRY.**

  No!   Yes.

REG. She's prettyish. Nothing to write home about. Before all of this happened, he actually didn't even like her!

LYLE. Didn't like her?

HENRY. She bothered me, yes, because she's a lot of work, and I went through everything I hate about her so many times, in my head, that I decided I like the things I hate about her.

LYLE. Is that the same thing as loving her?

HENRY. I never said "love."

LYLE. That's hardly a denial.

REG. Oh now he's in love with her.

LYLE. It does happen, Reg.

REG. Not in our family. And not in his either apparently now that he's made the stunning decision to have sex with both generations of Johnson women.

HENRY. How many times do I have to say it, I was being polite!

REG. You were drunk.

HENRY. Drunk and polite.

REG. What the fuck is wrong with you? Rene is like her mom! You don't fuck the mom, you don't fuck the sister, the best friend –

HENRY. Oh come on –

REG. Okay the best friend now and then but not Rene. They're both pissed. You fucked up and Rene will never let you near Mae again.

HENRY. *(To* **LYLE**.*)* Listen. Can I borrow you? Reg, can I borrow your cousin?

REG. Sure, I don't care.

LYLE. You want to "borrow" me? What for?

> *(He is somewhat amused by the idea. They consider each other.)*

Scene Five

WAITRESS. I love the Hamptons. It is so amazing to be here. I mean, the weather is just awesome and the beaches are totally incredible, the ocean is insane, and okay it's really expensive? I mean, like, you have to work maybe six jobs, just to be able to live in a not so great really tiny room in a house with seven other people in sort of a bad part of Bridgehampton or Amagansett or, you know, Quog? But it is worth it. The people who come here, there are so many who are just gorgeous and young and hot and happening the GLAMOUR. It's actually true! It's exactly what you'd think it would be but BETTER. Because you know what? They are really RICH. These people are so so so so so rich. And classy. Seriously it is pretty awesome here.

Scene Six

> (**MAE** *with an iPhone. She and* **RENE** *are shopping.)*

MAE. Have you ever heard of Lyle Swofford?

RENE. Swofford? Benjamin Swofford?

MAE. No, Lyle.

> *(They arrive at a restaurant.)*

RENE. The Dakota? The Atherton? There's a Swofford in the Village of all places. Alexa Swofford. Three townhouses, she bought out the neighbors and was apparently planning on joining the properties but the landmarks people put a stop to that, and she was left holding fifteen million in loans when the market crashed. Oops.

MAE. This is Lyle. He's from Boston. And he wants to meet you.

RENE. Why?

MAE. Reg says he saw your picture online at that MoMA benefit and he wants to meet you.

RENE. He wants to "meet" me? What does he look like?

MAE. I'm trying to find out.

> *(She is searching on her iPhone for a photo online.)*

RENE. Not that I am looking. I am finished with all that. The leap of the heart. The promise of joy. The yearning for ecstasy. That is no longer anything I'm interested in. Make sure this Lyle whoever knows that... Two!

MAE. I think he just wants to come to the party.

RENE. You said he wanted to meet me.

MAE. Yes, that's what Reg said.

RENE. But he's not from the Dakota or the Atherton or the Village.

MAE. No, he's from Boston.

RENE. *(A groan.)* Boston? Oh my god. Really? Boston? I don't think so darling. I don't think we want to invite a lot of extra people. This is meant to be intimate. And it's for you, to get over your broken heart.

MAE. *(Takes out Haiti travel guide from purse and begins to read.)* My heart isn't broken!

RENE. That's right. Your heart ISN'T broken.

MAE. It's really not, Aunt Rene. YOUR heart is broken.

RENE. Your heart isn't a little broken?

MAE. No!

RENE. Then neither of us have broken hearts! Good! Good for us! To hell with men.

MAE. Yes. Okay.

RENE. We defy them all!

MAE. Good. So, I'll tell Reg you don't want to meet this Lyle person.

RENE. Boston. What does he do?

MAE. Reg didn't say. They're cousins. He has a place on Nantucket but they're doing some renovations so he's here for a few weeks.

RENE. *(More impressed.)* Nantucket? Oh yes ooooh the Nantucket Swoffords, oooh, you didn't say that.

MAE. I think they're the same Swoffords as the Boston Swoffords.

RENE. How old is he? I'm done with younger men.

MAE. I thought you were done with all men, Aunt Rene –

RENE. What does he look like?

MAE. It doesn't matter what he looks like if he's not coming.

RENE. You are always so serious! Don't you at least want to know what he looks like?

MAE. No, to hell with men.

RENE. We should at least know what we're rejecting. It will make our stance all the more cunning.

MAE. Except what if he's ugly. Then there's no fun in rejecting him. And all men.

RENE. Is he ugly?

MAE. I don't know; I haven't seen a picture of him.

RENE. Well, that's what I mean, let's find one.

> (**MAE** *thinks about this, frustrated, slams down book.*)

What?

MAE. I – you know, I – I I don't want to go to a PARTY. I want to go somewhere and FEED THE POOR. I want to build HOUSING for the HOMELESS. I want – to find a village somewhere and work in an ORPHANAGE. I want to build a WATER PLANT.

RENE. Water plant. Oh, sweetheart. Is that really what you want? Come on, let's find a picture of this person. To hell with men!

> (*She smiles at* **MAE**.)

Scene Seven

WAITRESS. Shopping is very serious in the Hamptons. Everything you look at in a shop, or a boutique, is extremely beautiful and valuable. There are things that you think oh maybe that is too much money to pay for something, like fourteen hundred dollars for a pair of strappy sandals which anyone could buy something that looked like that at the Payless Shoes for thirty-seven dollars, and who could tell the difference, you could totally be wearing the cutest shoes ever for next to no money. You might think that. But the difference is in the essence. It's in the experience. It's value. And you know who could tell the difference? They could.

> *(She turns. She is now a* **SHOPGIRL.***)*

> *(A rack of beautiful women's clothing.* **KATRINA** *and* **MAE.** **MAE** *is wearing a hat. She looks at it in the mirror.)*

KATRINA. That is so cute.

MAE. I feel like some kind of deranged flower.

KATRINA. It's adorable!

MAE. It's two thousand dollars.

KATRINA. Well, you've earned it.

MAE. No one on Earth has earned a two-thousand-dollar hat, Katrina.

KATRINA. Mae. I refuse to let you feel shitty about a hat that cute. You can feel shitty because your boyfriend cheated on you. But the ultra-cute hat has been put on this earth to fix that.

MAE. He isn't my boyfriend.

KATRINA. Not anymore, obviously. It is so hilarious you didn't invite him to the party. Reg says he's really bugged by it.

MAE. I doubt that.

KATRINA. No it's the perfect revenge.

MAE. It was Rene's idea.

KATRINA. Why am I not surprised.

MAE. And he was not my boyfriend. He was never my boyfriend! We never called it that. It was different than that.

KATRINA. What do you mean?

MAE. It was just different. It was different from everything.

KATRINA. Mae. Are you in love with him?

(**MAE** *starts to cry.*)

No no no. No crying. No crying, you're wearing a really cute hat. Think about the hat.

MAE. I'm sorry.

(*She hands it to* **KATRINA.***)*

KATRINA. He was just after your money!

MAE. If he was after my money then why would he do what he did? Rene won't let him near me now.

KATRINA. She shouldn't.

MAE. I know. I know!

KATRINA. And she wouldn't let him near you before, either. You're just back where you started.

MAE. *(Honest, sad.)* If I were back where I started I would call him up and invite him to my party and think about what I was going to wear and hope that he thought I was pretty.

KATRINA. Mae listen to me. Everybody who meets him wants to sleep with Henry, and he likes it like that. Those guys are out there, they're everywhere, and they've been there since the dawn of time. Casanova. Don Juan. Leonardo DiCaprio. Everybody just wants to have sex with those guys all the time. It's like Donald Trump.

MAE. Donald Trump?

KATRINA. Yeah how would he ever know if anyone loved him for himself?

MAE. Well, I think he's got to assume that no one would.

KATRINA. That's my point. Love doesn't fit into all that. They don't even know what it is.

MAE. I don't think I want this hat.

KATRINA. Well I think it's totally reckless. I'm going to buy it.

> *(She puts it on and leaves.)*

> *(**CHARLES** and **HENRY** enter. They are trying on jackets.)*

Scene Eight

CHARLES. I'm just not crazy about the cut. I like a linen jacket, I'm never going to turn my nose up at linen, but they're always trying to put you in a size too large, like linen means loose, or without structure. And if you look at it, through history? The opposite is the case.

> *(Then:)*

Of course you look fabulous in linen.

HENRY. No, you're right. It's sloppy.

> *(He takes it off.)*

CHARLES. The color is fantastic.

HENRY. What's so fantastic about white?

CHARLES. It's vanilla.

HENRY. What's so fantastic about vanilla?

CHARLES. Okay, call it buttermilk. Eggshell. No wait, meringue?!

HENRY. Seriously?

CHARLES. Somebody's in a bad mood.

HENRY. Charles, could you –

CHARLES. What? Could I what?

> *(A beat.)*

HENRY. Nothing.

> *(He is straightening out his tie, his shirtsleeves. He is clearly pissed.)*

CHARLES. So.

> *(A beat.)*

Where are we having dinner?

HENRY. I have plans.

CHARLES. Oh. Who with?

HENRY. "With" someone else.

CHARLES. Do I know him?

HENRY. No, as a matter of fact you don't know her.

CHARLES. That's classic.

HENRY. "I'm having dinner with someone else" is classic? Maybe it's just a fact. I'm having dinner, with someone else. It's not like linen jackets and whether or not they're cut right. It's just a fucking fact. I'm having dinner with someone else. I have a date.

CHARLES. Well, we know who it's not with. Katrina told me you were left off the invite list for the big party at Mae's.

HENRY. You're gossiping about me? I'm touched.

CHARLES. It's the Hamptons. No one is beneath notice.

HENRY. That is not actually true. There are plenty of people who no one gossips about. "Beneath notice" is in fact a category. Surely you're aware of it.

(It's a dig.)

CHARLES. Was that meant to be funny?

HENRY. Did you laugh?

CHARLES. Why don't you just tell me who you're having dinner with? I'll know anyway. Within minutes, even.

HENRY. I'm sorry Charles. I feel bad. I didn't realize you were counting on me. You really don't have anything to do tonight?

(A beat.)

CHARLES. Maybe I'll call Mae. We can sit around and speculate, who you're fucking, now that she's cut you loose.

*(**HENRY** takes the hit.)*

HENRY. That sounds like a lot of fun.

*(He goes. **CHARLES** is pissed.)*

CHARLES. Asshole.

(He stalks off.)

Scene Nine

WAITRESS. I have to run to my second job now. My third job. Doesn't matter. I work in this really hot restaurant on Tuesdays and Fridays. The food is fantastic in the Hamptons. Everything is fresh. Vegetables come from the earth. The fish come from the sea. The fruit comes from the sky. That's just a little joke, obviously everything is locally sourced when it can be but things like mangoes and pineapples don't grow on Long Island, so they fly that in from Mexico. Because you cannot make a mango mojito without mango! And the drinks here are so important. They are the beating heart of the party scene so trust me, they are impeccable. Astonishing colors, purple and green and pink and bright blue. I know one bartender who can make a cocktail that changes colors while you drink it! I had a little crush on him. It didn't work out because there is, people here are very aware of who you are and where you fit and bartenders are like rock stars, sort of, they are very elite. So that didn't work out. But let me tell you, when the bars and the restaurants get going, it is wild, everyone is having such an amazing time. It doesn't matter if you are lonely at all.

(She exits.)

Scene Ten

*(RENE getting ready for the party. She is
wearing something truly fabulous, but she
can't get the scarf to work. MAE trails her.)*

RENE. I hate scarves. I hate them. This whole outfit makes
me look dumpy. Everything I own looks terrible on
me. This jacket cost eleven thousand dollars and I look
fat in it. I have thousands of dollars worth of clothes
in my closet and I can't wear any of them because no
one cares, they all hate women who are, I'm not saying
old. I am not old. I am not a teenager it's true. But this
whole culture has abandoned women over a certain
age, there is nothing for us, our couture choices are you
have to weigh sixty-eight pounds or you're consigned
to polyester. Polyester, with short sleeves. Powder blue
polyester with short sleeves. These are my choices! I
don't look good in anything.

MAE. That dress is gorgeous on you. You don't need the
jacket.

RENE. You haven't even left your twenties. You don't know
anything about what happens to women.

MAE. It's a different world now, Aunt Rene. No one cares
if if if –

RENE. If what, if you're hideous-looking?

MAE. You're not!

RENE. What do you know. He's coming to meet me because
of a photo that he saw online, I don't look anything like
that. Some idiot in a publicist's office had it touched
up. I haven't looked that good in fifteen years. And now
nothing, I've been through menopause! There, I've said
it. And what does that mean, that means I'll end my
life alone. I'm alone! And nothing fits.

MAE. Aunt Rene people are coming.

RENE. Meaning what, meaning I should humiliate myself,
wear something that looks ridiculous on me, to make
them feel superior! No. I won't do it. I'll go to Paris,

first, and hide, in an international cosmopolitan world center, where people are civilized and no one acts like you're an embarrassment just because you had a rough couple of weeks, and gained a few pounds.

MAE. People are here. You have to come down!

RENE. I'm not coming down. I can't take being humiliated again.

MAE. That shithead Henry is not going to be here, Aunt Rene, you were very careful to invite everyone on Long Island except for him. This isn't going to be humiliating, it's going to be a triumph. To hell with men!

RENE. "To hell with men" only works if you're wearing something fabulous.

MAE. And you are wearing something very fabulous. And we're throwing this party to show everyone that that to hell with men, our hearts are not broken, I certainly don't need a man and neither do you. It's a new world.

RENE. Oh dear. Didn't anyone tell you? Feminism is dead, darling. They keep trying to resurrect it, but it's not going to take.

MAE. *(Stern.)* Aunt Rene! We both of us have a ton of money. We're dripping with money! And we have vision. We are not victims!

RENE. I never said I was a victim.

MAE. Then stop acting like one!

RENE. I am not acting like a victim.

MAE. No you're not and you know why? Because you look fantastic in that ensemble.

RENE. *(Thinking.)* Wait, wait, wait. The hat alone cost six thousand dollars.

MAE. And nobody wears it better than you.

RENE. Do you really think so?

MAE. Aunt Rene. There are a lot of people downstairs. Including Lyle Swofford from Nantucket. He has come here to see what a six-thousand-dollar hat looks like on a real woman.

RENE. Real, what does "real" mean? Is that code for fat?

MAE. "Real" means "devastating."

RENE. All of it, or is the hat too much?

MAE. All of it. Including the hat.

> *(She holds it up.* RENE *takes it, puts it on with real flair. She goes off.* MAE *follows her, exhausted.)*

Scene Eleven

(The **WAITRESS** *with a plate of hors d'oeuvres.)*

WAITRESS. The parties are the best part of being out here. You sign up with a catering company and you don't know when they're going to call, sometimes you don't get called till the total last minute and you have to be ready to show up when they do that or you go to the bottom of the list. It's a very hard gig to get because you have to be totally reliable. The people giving the party, they are the hosts! You do not talk to them. They are entertaining their guests, some of whom are like, important or famous, and you have to be completely cool about it, like you can't stare or ask for an autograph or even just say, "Oh I think your movies are so amazing," that is NOT. I can't even tell you some of the people who I have waited on. I know somebody though who served a party that the First Lady was at, and there were Secret Service guys everywhere, with guns, it sounded crazy – like, not crazy, but really like intense. Anyway, it's not usually like that, usually you're just, you have to be as I said reliable and pleasant and you know, invisible.

(The party. She turns to **KATRINA**, **REG**, **CHARLES**, *and* **LYLE**, *who have just arrived.)*

A mini potato pancake with seared tuna tartar and balsamic demi-glaze.

KATRINA. No thanks. Too many carbs.

REG. It's the size of a postage stamp.

KATRINA. So why eat it?

LYLE. This place is gorgeous. I don't think I've ever seen a lawn that green.

CHARLES. You know the story, right?

LYLE. The story about grass?

CHARLES. They paint it.

LYLE. They paint it?

CHARLES. Absolutely, they paint it green.

LYLE. It's not green by itself?

CHARLES. Not green enough.

LYLE. They paint the grass.

CHARLES. You see all those Mexicans out there, in khakis and pink shirts?

LYLE. Those are Mexicans?

CHARLES. Those are Mexicans who are painting the grass.

KATRINA. Those are guests.

CHARLES. They have little spray cans.

KATRINA. If they are painting the grass, it's because we're early. They'll stop any minute. Look. They're stopping.

CHARLES. Oh Jesus.

LYLE. Do they paint the flowers, too?

KATRINA. They might, but I haven't heard of that. Charles stop making that face. This is not new news. The sun is strong out here, if the grass needs a little help, so be it.

CHARLES. Or the women.

KATRINA. Oh like men don't have plastic surgery. That's hilarious.

(RENE *enters, followed by* MAE.)

RENE. Hello. Hello everyone.

REG. Rene! You look devastating, as usual.

RENE. Darling Reg. I'm so glad you could stop by.

KATRINA. Rene, that hat is amazing!

(*Everyone starts kissing.*)

CHARLES. Rene! We were just watching them paint the grass.

MAE. I know it's stupid.

RENE. It's hardly stupid. It really improves the look of the lawn. And call me crazy but it's important to me, to keep people employed. I take that responsibility really seriously and I don't apologize for it. Honestly, I am tired of people saying that the one percent doesn't do enough. I really am.

REG. Rene, I want you to meet my cousin, Lyle.

RENE. Hello, Lyle.

LYLE. Thank you so much for including me, Rene.

RENE. Oh of course! When Reg said you were in town, I said, darling, please, you must bring him. Truth be told we may have met before. At the Nantucket Wine Festival, two years ago? I was there visiting Leslie and Dick Sylvester.

LYLE. Oh, I haven't seen Dick and Leslie in years.

RENE. They look wonderful.

LYLE. They always do.

RENE. How long are you in town?

LYLE. For a while. They're doing some renovation on our place, so I'm camping out with Reg here at his place in Amagansett.

RENE. Well, I hope to see more of you.

LYLE. I'm counting on it. I love it here! Nantucket is really drab by comparison. All those whales.

RENE. Whales are endangered. And they're very intelligent.

LYLE. Trust me, you can get tired of them. And scrimshaw. And all those gray shingles. The Hamptons are so full of light by comparison. There's energy here. And color.

RENE. We have history too!

LYLE. Perhaps. But right now I am more taken by the beauty.

(*He smiles at* **RENE.** *She is overwhelmed.*)

You know, if it's not too much to ask, I'd love to see the grounds.

RENE. I'd love to show them to you!

(*He offers her his arm. She takes it. They go, passing the* **WAITRESS,** *who carries drinks.*)

CHARLES. Look out for the paint!

MAE. (*To* **REG.**) Reg, he better be a gentleman.

REG. Lyle? Shit yeah. He's awesome.

MAE. You're sure? Because honestly it means a lot to her, that someone might show a little interest in her, and so she is excited to meet him and I hope he's not an asshole.

REG. No, he's not an asshole.

> (**MAE** *doesn't sincerely seem to think so.*)

MAE. What does he do?

REG. You know, what do any of us do?

MAE. That's a little vague, Reg.

REG. Well, yeah, but we're all a little vague, when you get down to it.

> (*The* **WAITRESS** *approaches.*)

WAITRESS. These are asparagus spears marinated in a lime yogurt cilantro dressing and sautéed with red pepper – um. Red pepper sauté. I'm sorry, a red pepper reduction. Sorry.

> (**CHARLES** *and* **KATRINA** *take a few steps apart, watching* **LYLE** *and* **RENE** *in the distance.*)

These are asparagus spears marinated in a lime yogurt cilantro dressing and sautéed with a red pepper reduction.

KATRINA. Is it vegan?

WAITRESS. It's vegetarian, yes.

KATRINA. Vegan. Vegan.

WAITRESS. Oh –

CHARLES. It's not vegan. There's yogurt.

WAITRESS. Yes, there's yogurt in the dressing.

KATRINA. Is it non-dairy?

WAITRESS. Non-dairy yogurt, I'll ask.

CHARLES. She's pulling your leg. There's no such thing.

KATRINA. (*To* **CHARLES**.) There's soy.
(*To the* **WAITRESS**.) Is it soy yogurt?

WAITRESS. Oh. I don't know.

KATRINA. It's fine.

WAITRESS. I'm sorry.

KATRINA. Can you ask the kitchen if there's anything vegan?

WAITRESS. Absolutely.

KATRINA. Thank you.

> (*The* **WAITRESS** *goes.* **KATRINA** *looks out at* **LYLE** *and* **RENE.**)

So what's his name? Lyle?

CHARLES. Lyle Swofford.

KATRINA. Lyle Swofford.

REG. (*Mocking* **KATRINA.**) "Lyle Swofford." He's my cousin. I told you about him.

KATRINA. Yes you did.

REG. He's staying at my house, I told you this.

KATRINA. Yes you did Reg, I remember. I just think it's awfully convenient that he showed up.

CHARLES. Convenient?

KATRINA. Yes, Reg. You have a convenient cousin. I find that strange.

> (*The* **WAITRESS** *returns with a new tray.* **KATRINA, CHARLES, REG,** *and* **MAE** *go to see what she has.*)

WAITRESS. Spiced slippery tofu in a rice wine vinegar, baked in a gluten-free puff pastry.

MAE. I love these.

WAITRESS. I'll tell the chef.

MAE. (*To* **CHARLES.**) You should have one, they're delicious.

CHARLES. Gluten-free makes me nervous.

MAE. Really?

REG. (*Eating.*) No, it tastes okay.

MAE. I think they're delicious.

REG. That's what I mean. They are fucking delicious, Mae.

MAE. Thanks, Reg.

REG. (*To* **KATRINA.**) You should have one. They're like vegan everything free, right?

WAITRESS. Absolutely.

KATRINA. Are there peanuts?

WAITRESS. Oh, I – I don't know. They didn't say anything about peanuts.

KATRINA. Peanut oil?

WAITRESS. No. No!

KATRINA. Could you ask?

REG. Since when did you become allergic to peanuts?

KATRINA. It's not an allergy. But there's definitely a sensitivity.

REG. You're sensitive to peanuts?

CHARLES. I understand that because I have always been completely offended by them.

WAITRESS. I'll totally ask.

KATRINA. That would be totally lovely. Because it would be awesome if there was something I could actually eat at this party.

WAITRESS. Yes. I'm sorry. Yes.

> (*She turns to hurry off.*)

KATRINA. I don't know where they find people like that.

> (*The* **WAITRESS** *runs right into* **HENRY**. *The plate of tofu things goes flying.*)

WAITRESS. I'm sorry, I'm so so so sorry.

KATRINA. (*Overlap.*) What on earth.

HENRY. (*Overlap.*) My fault. It's my fault –

> (**KATRINA** *stops when she realizes it's* **HENRY.**)

So so so so sorry.

> (*He helps the* **WAITRESS** *put the food back on the tray.*)

Seriously I am so sorry.

WAITRESS. It's my fault. It's totally my fault. I am so so sorry.

*(Mortified, she goes. **HENRY** looks after her.)*

HENRY. Poor thing. Seriously, it was completely my fault.

(They all stare at him.)

Can I get a drink?

*(**REG** moves to give **HENRY** his drink.)*

MAE. *(Stopping him.)* Reg.

*(To **CHARLES**.)* Charles, would you go get one of the valet parking attendants? Get a couple of them. We have an intruder.

HENRY. Mae, I know you're mad at me.

MAE. I'm not mad at you. I have too much money to bother thinking about anyone who doesn't and oh! That includes you, doesn't it?

HENRY. That seems rather cruel.

MAE. One's cruelty is one's power; and when one parts with one's cruelty one parts with one's power; and when one has parted with that I fancy one's old and ugly. Know where I learned that? From you.

HENRY. You have to give me just one minute to explain what happened.

MAE. Explanations are for people who care, from people who don't.

HENRY. Explanations are facts which have been annihilated by gossip.

MAE. It's not gossip when it actually happened. Things that happened are the truth.

HENRY. The truth is overrated.

MAE. So is having sex with you.

KATRINA. Snap.

MAE. There is not so impudent a thing in nature as the saucy look of an assured man confident of success. Want to know where I learned that? From him.

HENRY. This is a rather extreme reaction to a situation you haven't even let me clarify.

MAE. Clarity relies on assumptions which are rarely true.

HENRY. Such as?

MAE. I think we can start with the assumption that I care about anything you have to say, under any circumstances, now or ever.

HENRY. You gave me some reason to believe that you did.

MAE. Why? One makes lovers as fast as one pleases and they live as long as one pleases and they die as soon as one pleases, and then if one pleases one makes more. Want to know where I learned that?

HENRY. Okay. If we're going to really talk about this, could we go someplace else?

REG.	**CHARLES & KATRINA.**
No.	No no no no no.

HENRY. We could use a little privacy.

MAE. Why should conversation be private when nothing else is?

HENRY. It is the heart that is private. Isn't it?

MAE. Since you actually don't have one, I'm going to assume you're just venturing a guess here.

HENRY. A woman whose heart is safe has no need to throw away her fortune.

MAE. Meaning what?

HENRY. Meaning –

MAE. Don't answer that. I'm not interested.
Where are those valet parking guys? Where are the guys who paint the lawn? Will someone get someone who knows how to actually DO something to come in here and remove this person? Reg, call the police if you have to.

HENRY. You don't want to do that. Please Mae. Just one moment alone. You know it's what you want.

MAE. Henry, I won't say it's not fun, watching you grovel. But, if you're trying to suck up to a girl, don't tell her you know what she's thinking. Boys tell us that all the time and you know what? We don't like it.

CHARLES. Snap again.

MAE. You vastly overestimate your influence on the cosmic order, Henry. You think I want to give away my money because you broke my heart? Let me explain something. If I give away my money it will have nothing to do with you. The stars will have more to say about it. Would anyone want to go see the pool? It is so pretty in the moonlight.

> *(She goes.* **CHARLES,** *raising an eyebrow, follows.* **REG** *and* **KATRINA** *follow. The* **WAITRESS** *enters with a tray of drinks, and* **HENRY** *drinks one. Then another. And another. The* **WAITRESS** *goes.* **KATRINA** *re-enters. She looks around, goes to* **HENRY.***)*

KATRINA. You okay?

HENRY. What do you think?

KATRINA. I think you should let me take you home.

> *(She puts her hand on his arm seductively.)*

HENRY. Oh what the hell.

> *(He looks at her. She looks at him. He grabs her in an embrace. They kiss. He dips her mid-kiss. The kiss gets really hot.)*

ACT TWO

Scene One

(The **WAITRESS.***)*

WAITRESS. The houses out here are incredible. I mean, I know that's like stating the obvious, you can just drive around like on the streets here and see, that they're all huge and gorgeous and like that, but I get to see inside. Where they live their lives. The kitchens – where seriously the appliances are so beautiful – and the pool house and the living rooms, some of the living rooms are like, these huge open rooms that are just PERFECT. Perfect furniture. Perfect windows. Perfect lamps. The carpets! Oh my gosh. Also there are screening rooms. Where like you know total movie moguls live in these houses, and they have their own room, with a giant movie screen and a popcorn machine! I'm not making this up. So you can watch, anything you want, and sit on a gorgeous couch, and then you have your popcorn. And that's not even, that's like just the first floor. The upstairs, there are hallways and bathrooms that are so amazing heated tiles on the floor which I don't know why you would have that honestly because most people don't come here at all, the rest of the year, when maybe it's a little cooler, but I think people do the heated tile floor just in case and because it's you know it's just what they do. One house I worked at there was a personal gym up there with all new equipment and a trainer! He was just sitting there. And bedrooms. And the bedrooms – look. Look!

Scene Two

*(A giant bed. **HENRY** is in it with **KATRINA**. They are having mind-blowing sex.)*

(They finish.)

KATRINA. That was – oh my god. That was amazing. Magical. Fantastic.

*(**HENRY** gets up, starts dressing.)*

You really are gorgeous.

*(**HENRY** continues to dress.)*

Do you have to go?

*(**HENRY** continues to dress.)*

Henry, don't you think you could at least pretend that we just had really great sex and that you actually like me, so that I don't feel like a total whore?

HENRY. Sorry. I'm just in my head. You're not a total whore.

KATRINA. Oh thanks.

HENRY. You're the one who said it!

KATRINA. I hate you.

HENRY. I know you do.

(He gives her a long, lingering kiss and goes, leaving her in bed.)

Scene Three

> (**KATRINA** *falls back in the bed. It is the next day.*)

KATRINA. I HATE HIM.

> (**CHARLES** *enters with a bottle of vodka, pours her a drink.*)

CHARLES. I'm not the one who told you to sleep with him.

> (**KATRINA** *drinks and gets dressed.*)

KATRINA. You don't act like that. You don't have sex with someone who you've known for years, someone you've been inVOLVED with, and then just walk away. Okay maybe you do? But it makes you a lousy person. I am well aware that he was angry at Mae for publicly humiliating him like that, and that coming home with me was not a complete declaration of love, or anything. I mean, I am not naive. I realize he was – using me, and I was using him! I participated. But it was because I was trying to help. Because I do, I care about him and I think he is wasting his time, obsessing on Mae. Who will never take him back. She's so moral. She might as well be a Midwesterner. Seriously, whatever she is, I don't see it. It doesn't grab me. She is a friend, I like her, and I admire her, and I understand the appeal of the whole six hundred million, but the rest of it escapes me. I'm just being honest. And I was trying to help him get over that, and you know what? He could just make a fucking phone call. You have sex with someone, you should call, the next day. That's all I'm saying.

CHARLES. So he didn't call.

KATRINA. What have I been saying. No! He didn't call. He didn't spend the night and then he didn't call.

CHARLES. Okay. I'm your friend?

KATRINA. Oh my God, don't say that. Whenever you say you're my friend, I know you're about to say something truly hideous.

CHARLES. Seriously I am your friend. But if you are just having rebound sex with someone, and you know that going in, you can't expect him to call.

KATRINA. I can and I do expect him to call.

CHARLES. Even though he's in love with someone else.

KATRINA. He is not in love with her! She has too much money for anyone ever to know if they love her. And what's more she knows that. Plus, she hates him.

CHARLES. Plus you hate him.

KATRINA. I completely hate him. He's disgusting, really, if you think about it. Aside from being really hot and great in bed, who cares about Henry?

CHARLES. But you still want him to call.

KATRINA. I don't want him to call. I'm just saying, he should have.

CHARLES. Women are stupid, about the phone. Men don't like the phone. Because they don't want to communicate. They don't need to communicate.
Why would he need to communicate? He just got laid. This is why men and women will never get along. It really is.

KATRINA. Charles, can I just say something? You're gay. You're sooooo gay, and you're in love with a straight man. So don't tell me how stupid women are, about the phone. You may know what men think about the phone? But you know nothing about anything else.

CHARLES. I know nothing.

KATRINA. You know nothing about straight men.

CHARLES. I know more than you think.

KATRINA. You think they're all gay, it makes you retarded and stupid because they're NOT secretly gay, THEY'RE STRAIGHT.

CHARLES. I'm so uninterested in this discussion.

KATRINA. You know what I don't get? How he knew Rene was not going to be there. There's no way he could have even gotten near Mae, much less had a conversation with her if Rene was around. But she was very conveniently preoccupied with this Lyle character.

CHARLES. You think he's a fraud?

KATRINA. No, I looked him up online, he's real.

CHARLES. Oh. You "looked him up"?

KATRINA. It's called Googling, and everybody does it.

CHARLES. Googling?

KATRINA. There's something wrong with him.

CHARLES. Katrina. There's something wrong with all of us.

(He pours her another drink. Lights shift.)

Scene Four

*(**REG** and **HENRY** having drinks.)*

REG. So that thing at the party, with Mae? Epic. What a disaster. I mean wow. What a train wreck. What a titanic failure. What a humiliation.

HENRY. It's fine.

REG. Dude it wasn't fine.

HENRY. *(To the **WAITRESS**.)* I think we're going to need another round.

*(The **WAITRESS** nods and goes.)*

REG. I got your back, bro.

HENRY. Thanks.

REG. But maybe it's time to, you know.

*(**HENRY** looks at him.)*

Widen your perspective.

HENRY. My perspective?

REG. Don't get me wrong. It was bold. It was bold, what you did. And women like that. You know they want to know that you won't give up after one total fuckup. But when they take you down like that? You're on life support, man. Honestly you're not even on life support. You've flatlined.

HENRY. I'm so glad you called me to have a drink with you this afternoon, Reg. I really appreciate it.

REG. *(Taking **HENRY**'s hand.)* Henry, we're men. We got to stick together.

HENRY. Can I have my hand back?

REG. *(Dropping **HENRY**'s hand.)* Yeah. Do you want my advice?

HENRY. I don't actually.

REG. Give up on Mae. Because she is like, she is like Moby Dick. Moby Dick! Dude, it's an American classic.

HENRY. I've heard of it.

REG. Yeah, so this guy Ahab, Moby Dick chews off his leg.

HENRY. I've heard of it, Reg.

REG. And Ahab's like "ow." But Moby Dick owns him. He owns his heart. Ahab is an emotional cripple.

HENRY. I'm not an emotional cripple.

REG. Dude I'm just talking to you about Moby Dick! Ahab just won't give it up. And so he dies. Moby Dick kills him. He eats him. He eats his dick.

HENRY. What's your point, Reg?

REG. My point is, Don't Die. And don't get your dick eaten.

> *(The* **WAITRESS** *shows up, starts switching out drinks.)*

HENRY. I think you better just keep them coming.

> *(He drains his drink. The* **WAITRESS** *nods. Blackout.)*

Scene Five

> *(Rene's bedroom.* **RENE** *enters with* **LYLE**. *They carry drinks.)*
>
> *(They are both wearing dazzling clothing. The light is gorgeous. It is sunset.)*

LYLE. I love all the little touches, the vases, the *objects* –

RENE. Oh I have so many treasures. Seriously, it's a passion with me. The *object*. There's one in particular I want to show you – I think it's in here. The master bedroom.

LYLE. Your house is spectacular, Rene.

RENE. I did everything myself. The painting, the wallpaper, everything.

LYLE. You – painted, and –

RENE. Oh, no, sorry. *(Laughing.)* I hired a decorator who picked the paint colors and the wallpaper and then he hired people to do the rest.

LYLE. I love those people. They're so handy.

RENE. Oh, I couldn't live without them. And I have to say I really resent people saying we don't do enough, for the other ninety-nine percent. You look around the Hamptons and you can just see the truth of it. We are the job creators. We are! Taxing us and asking us to pay our "fair share" is ridiculous. We pay our fair share! By employing people.

LYLE. I can personally testify to that. We are employing dozens out on Nantucket. They are rebuilding the family shack one shingle at a time.

RENE. That's wonderful!

LYLE. Is it?

RENE. Your family heritage must be important to you.

> *(She sits on the bed, leans up against the pillows.)*

As it should be! You, we, are the curators of the American legacy. Our special attention and care, lavished on these historic homes, is part of our gift to culture. Which is another way we contribute.

LYLE. Your mind is amazing.

RENE. Which is why you like me.

LYLE. But Rene when was the last time you visited Nantucket?

RENE. Let's go tomorrow!

LYLE. Let's not. You laugh but seriously it is not the Hamptons. You don't know what you have here.

RENE. *(Breathless.)* I think I do.

> *(She looks at him with unabashed lust. He checks his watch.)*

LYLE. I probably should be going.

RENE. Oh don't! We're having such a lovely time. And I haven't shown you half the house – and all my little treasures, that you like so much. What did we even come up here to see, the Tiffany jade or my little Dresden shepherdess, I can't remember –

LYLE. I can see it, and the rest of the house another time. Seriously, you've been so generous.

RENE. Don't say that. It's not generosity. I'm not generous at all, really, I'm just so happy to have someone truly fascinating with whom I might share the secrets of my heart. No no no – Oh, I remember – you must see it, it's right here in my dressing room, it is such a cunning little amuse-bouche, I only show it to my special friends.

> *(She goes. **LYLE** looks out the window. He checks his watch. After a moment, **MAE** enters.)*

MAE. Aunt Rene do you want to go to this art opening Katrina's – oh! I'm sorry. I didn't realize you were in here.

LYLE. She was just giving me the tour. It's a beautiful house.

MAE. Yes. It is.

LYLE. So many extraordinary little treasures.

MAE. Yes, she likes buying things. And she has really good taste. Which is good, because then the things she buys are all pretty fabulous. And I get it. I do. You've got to spend it on something. Honestly, I've got so much money. Have you heard?

LYLE. Yes.

MAE. I've got so much money, if you printed it all out, like in small bills, it could squash you. But the fact is I can't get myself to spend it. I'm tired of things. Stuff. You know. All this stuff that people buy with money, I'm kind of sick of it. Not kind of. Really sick of it. Really, really tired of stuff. Has that ever happened to you?

LYLE. No.

MAE. Don't you come from a big – your family –

LYLE. My family has a lot of money, yes, and we spend it recklessly and we buy a lot of things, and there's always more money. I've never gotten tired of that part of it.

MAE. Oh.

LYLE. Other parts.

> *(He shrugs, thinking about how exhausting the other parts are.)*

Listen. Could you tell Rene I'm sorry, but I really have to run.

> *(He starts to go.)*

MAE. Can't you tell her yourself?

LYLE. I'm just actually in such a hurry. I'll finish the tour next time.

MAE. You're not – listen, you're not –

> *(She stops herself.)*

LYLE. What?

MAE. Nothing.

> *(**LYLE** goes. **MAE** sits. After a moment, **RENE** re-enters. She wears a brilliant silk kimono over a daring negligee.)*

RENE. Well, I can't find it. No matter! It's the most dazzling little Fabergé spider brooch, truly rare and exceedingly controversial but I can't find it!

(Sees **MAE.***)*

Mae! Oh – darling. I'm sorry, I'm actually entertaining a friend right now.

MAE. Entertaining a friend. By "friend" do you mean Lyle Swofford?

RENE. Yes, I am! Oh darling he's fantastic. So deep, and passionate and very very sensitive, not to mention gorgeous, he's simply gorgeous! I'm enraptured, Mae, I really am. Did you see him? Did he step out for a moment, to refresh his cocktail?

MAE. Aunt Rene, you met him three days ago! You don't know this person.

RENE. Some people you know instantly. In your heart, you recognize a fellow traveler.

MAE. You were going to sleep with him. Weren't you?

RENE. Please don't put it in the past tense. I'm a little more optimistic than that.

MAE. After knowing him three days. You've never even been on an actual date!

RENE. Darling. Can we talk about this later. It's affecting my mood.

MAE. The whole world, everybody in the world is a slut! I live in a world of just – look at you! You'll sleep with anyone!

RENE. I will not sleep with anyone. I categorically deny it.

MAE. Aunt Rene, you were devastated. You slept with Henry once and then when it turned out to mean nothing you couldn't get out of bed. For days I listened to you complain about how horrible he was, because he didn't phone and you were all, he betrayed you and who needs men and that was THREE DAYS AGO. I am so stupid. I am really so so stupid.

RENE. Is that what this is about? Your crush?

MAE. He is not my crush.

RENE. Darling. I am sorry this is upsetting you. I know you had feelings for – that other young man, and that my involvement with him was problematic for you. I knew you were feeling a little bit jealous. I knew that and I was sorry about it, I really was. But it was a *coup de foudre*, a madness of the heart.

MAE. A what?!

RENE. But I think it's clear he is not to be trusted. With you OR your fortune.

MAE. I know, I know I know.

RENE. Darling I think I know a little bit more about men than you do. Now Mae, please don't take this wrong. Do you promise? Promise not to be mad at me, for what I say next? Promise?

MAE. How can I promise when I don't know what you're going to say?

RENE. This is my point. You are so rational. That's why you're having so much trouble with men. Don't deny it. We'll talk about it later. Right now, I really really really would just love it if we could table this discussion. Lyle is going to be back any moment. Although with all this yelling, I wouldn't be surprised if you had frightened him off!

MAE. He left, Aunt Rene.

RENE. He left?

MAE. Yes, he left! I came looking for you to ask you about this opening that Katrina wants us to go to, and he said he had to go and he left.

RENE. What did you say to him?

MAE. I didn't say anything! I didn't know he was in here, so I just came in and he said you were going to show him something but that he had plans and he'd see it later and he left.

RENE. What were his exact words?

MAE. Oh come on –

RENE. His exact words! Please!

MAE. I didn't take notes!

RENE. Well you should have!

*(She sits in a fury. **MAE** sighs.)*

MAE. He said he would come back. He said he loved the house. He loved seeing all your treasures. He apologized.

RENE. And he said he'd come back.

MAE. Yes, he did say that.

RENE. I did want to show him that silly little spider brooch. It might be Fabergé. If it isn't it's still nineteenth-century, and it's a gorgeous piece.

MAE. If you like pinning spiders to your chest.

RENE. Exactly so. Exactly so!

(More cheerful.) He said he'd come back.

MAE. He did.

RENE. Well. I will not let him out of my web again.

*(She laughs. **MAE** smiles. They go.)*

Scene Six

> (*The* **WAITRESS** *appears. She is in her underwear and a cute little t-shirt.*)

WAITRESS. Guess what happened to me? I got a boyfriend! Well, it's probably too soon to call him my "boyfriend," we've only slept together once but it was so so fun and he's really funny and nice. I was actually getting a little depressed because seriously I love it here? But I'm just going to say it: It's hard, like working so hard? When there are so many rich people around. I know that's like controversial? Because this is America and nobody wants it to be a socialist country, so if you don't have money, it's up to you to figure out how to make it, yourself, I know that. But sometimes – I'm working like six jobs, I already told you that, and I have a crazy long commute to some of them, and none of them really pay and you know what? Rich people are SHITTY TIPPERS. Not all of them, I'm not saying that, but when you're working like really hard, and people are not as nice as they might be, you know, a couple of bad tips really just takes the heart out of you.

> (*She starts to tear up, then stops herself.*)

I'm sorry. Sorry. Really I've just been working really hard. So I'm a little reactive.

> (*She wipes her eyes.*)

Anyway. I have a boyfriend! He's really nice. And he's cool, he's just – he's totally cool. And way hot in bed. So, that helps a lot.

> (**HENRY** *enters. He is in his underwear, and he carries something in his hand.*)

HENRY. What's this?

WAITRESS. What?

HENRY. I found this, in your purse.

> (*He holds up the spider brooch, and also the purse, which is frankly rather large.*)

WAITRESS. You were looking in my purse?

HENRY. I was trying to find a pen, so I could get your phone number.

WAITRESS. Well, why didn't you just ask?

HENRY. Because I didn't think that I was going to find the loot of a thousand worlds stuffed into a waitress's tote bag.

> *(He starts to dump it all over the bed. There is, in fact, a lot of loot in there.)*

WAITRESS. Those are, you know, that's my stuff.

HENRY. Is it?

> *(The* **WAITRESS** *looks at him, terrified, then tries to cover.)*

WAITRESS. It's totally my stuff.

HENRY. That's, okay. I didn't understand that. Most people don't carry hand-painted Limoges boxes around with them.

> *(The* **WAITRESS** *ducks her head into the purse, pulls out a pen.)*

WAITRESS. Here's a pen.

HENRY. Yes, the Montblanc Ingrid Bergman. It's very nice. It retails for three thousand dollars.

WAITRESS. How do you know?

HENRY. Oh, sweetheart. People like me know about Montblanc pens. You want to tell me about it?

> *(He gestures to the stuff, looks at the* **WAITRESS** *with sympathy. She takes a breath. Starts to cry, then confess.)*

WAITRESS. It's, I, there's just so many things! Everywhere. And I work so hard and they don't PAY ME. I, I didn't, the first time, it just kind of happened, it was an accident, not an accident, but it was just sort of, they would never know! It was like there was this big glass cabinet with all these things. And they would never know. If one was gone. And it was pretty. And I was tired. It was just a slip. It really was.

(**HENRY** *looks at the pile of stuff on her bed.*)

HENRY. This is more than one little slip.

(*He starts to get dressed.*)

WAITRESS. Well. Yes. When they didn't notice, the first time, I tried it a couple other times. And no one ever notices! What is the point of having all these things if you don't even know you have them? And I'm supposed to feel bad, for taking them?

HENRY. Do you feel bad?

WAITRESS. (*Catching herself.*) Yes. Of course. I feel terrible.

(*A beat.*)

HENRY. Really?

WAITRESS. No. I don't feel bad at all.

HENRY. Well maybe you want to practice. Because this thing here? Is an heirloom.

WAITRESS. Okay, I'm not stupid. Please do not think I'm stupid. What's an heirloom. Because I thought it was a tomato.

HENRY. It's old and valuable. It's been in the Johnson family for like a hundred years. It's worth like thirty thousand dollars.

WAITRESS. That's worth, come on.

HENRY. This is serious. This thing is real! Gold, and diamonds and rubies. There's no way they won't miss it. And when they do? They will call the cops, who will put two and two together. The rest of this stuff, you might get away with. This?

(*Holding up the brooch.*)

Is grand larceny. You're a jewel thief.

(*The **WAITRESS** is starting to panic a little.*)

WAITRESS. Are you going to turn me in?

HENRY. Are you kidding? What do I care? But I'm taking this, okay? I think I might be able to find a use for it.

(*He holds up the spider brooch, pockets it.*)

WAITRESS. And you won't tell anybody?

HENRY. No. But if I need you to do me a favor someday, I'm going to expect you to do it.

WAITRESS. Like what kind of favor?

HENRY. I'll know when I figure it out.

(*He shrugs on his sweater, kisses the* **WAITRESS**, *and goes.*)

Scene Seven

> (**LYLE** *and* **CHARLES** *in bed. They are having great sex.*)
>
> (*They finish.*)

LYLE. Fuck. That was great. That was so great.

> (*After a breathless moment* **CHARLES** *stretches and reaches for his khakis, pulls out a cell phone, and starts to check it.*)

Tell me you didn't just do that.

CHARLES. Sorry? Oh, sorry. I just need to check something out.

LYLE. I hate men.

> (*He gets out of bed and starts dressing.*)

CHARLES. Don't do that. Oh come on. Are you going to get all insecure on me?

LYLE. I'm not insecure. I'm very secure. I know who I am, and what I want. We had a good time. We had a great time at dinner and the sex, that sex we just had, was legitimately terrific. And you're so threatened, by what a good time we had you had to pretend, you had to make this totally passive-aggressive, you know what? I'm out of here. You're fucked up.

CHARLES. I'm fucked up?

LYLE. You hang out with straight people too much. You're probably in love with a straight guy, you have all the signs.

CHARLES. (*Snapping.*) I am not in love with –

> (*A beat.*)

LYLE. Guess I hit a nerve.

CHARLES. You don't know what you're talking about.

LYLE. Whatever.

CHARLES. And in any case you're not exactly, I "hang out with straight people too much"? Are you kidding me?

You're swanning all over the Hamptons with Rene Johnson on your arm. What's the story there, did you just fail to mention to her that you're gay? Is that how secure you are? Who picks up the check? Who pays for the clothes?

LYLE. I don't need anybody else to buy me clothes.

CHARLES. Then you're after bigger game! How many times do you think that you're going to have to screw her, to get a gold Mercedes? How many times for a Bentley?

LYLE. That's not – that is not what is going on –

CHARLES. Which is why you're sleeping in Reg's guest room.

(*He continues to text.* **LYLE** *watches him, then:*)

LYLE. You don't know what you're talking about. I came here – I came here, because I want my life to be different.

CHARLES. Guess what. It's not that different. In fact, we've all seen it a million times.

LYLE. I am not a gigolo, or a hustler.

CHARLES. Just a walker then? Leech? Suck-up? Oh, here's another word for it: Fag?

(**LYLE** *sits, thinking about this.*)

LYLE. I think – maybe – I deserve this.

CHARLES. (*Still texting.*) Why, did I hit a nerve?

LYLE. Your friend Henry asked me to be nice to her. I didn't see any harm in it. But of course she's misunderstood it. And of course I'm letting her.

(**CHARLES** *looks up at this.*)

CHARLES. Hang on. Henry asked you to –

LYLE. Just to be nice to her. To distract her a little, so that he had a chance to resolve this situation with the heiress, the niece.

CHARLES. "The niece"? Did he call her that?

LYLE. No of course not –

CHARLES. *(Delighted now.)* Henry put you up to this. He told you to "distract" Rene so he could –

LYLE. Yes. Yes!

> *(He is not proud of himself.* **CHARLES** *hoots with delight.)*

CHARLES. Katrina called this. She is hilarious. What an eye she has, it's impeccable. She knew there was something wrong, when you just showed up like that. She knew there was something fishy.

LYLE. Nothing happened!

CHARLES. Oh please. This is so not nothing. This is not nothing.

LYLE. Look, why do you care?

CHARLES. Are you kidding?

LYLE. No, I'm not kidding. We had a great time tonight. We should get out of here. Let's go to the Pines for the weekend. My treat. I really do have my own money. I have a lot of it.

CHARLES. Let me think about it.

LYLE. *(Knows it's a brush-off.)* Yeah. Okay. Anyway, thanks for the wake-up call.

CHARLES. What does that mean?

LYLE. It means you're right, it's lousy of me to let Rene think what she's thinking. I'm going to tell her the truth.

CHARLES. No no not – oh no. Don't do that.

LYLE. Why not?

CHARLES. Well, because – it will embarrass her! Seriously Rene is a rare flower, she's sensitive.

LYLE. I can't let her just keep thinking –

CHARLES. No, no of course not. I just mean, don't make a big thing. You can let her down easy, without telling her the whole story. Look, she's been humiliated enough already, don't you think? I think the woman deserves a shred of kindness.

LYLE. I like her.

CHARLES. I love her! It's disgraceful the way Henry has been manipulating her, and this whole situation. But why give up the information before you've figured out a use for it?

LYLE. What kind of "use"?

CHARLES. There just might be a way to play that card! Have some fun with it.

LYLE. You think this is fun.

CHARLES. You've been having fun all night, you just told me yourself.

LYLE. Well, I was until –

CHARLES. Until what? Don't go. Come on. We were having a good time. Don't go.

(A beat.)

LYLE. You're confusing.

CHARLES. Good.

(They kiss.)

Scene Eight

(The art show. **KATRINA**, **REG**, **LYLE**, *and* **CHARLES** *study a painting.)*

KATRINA. Do you get this? I don't get it.

REG. What are you talking about? You're the one who dragged us here!

KATRINA. As a favor to my sister! She's collecting art now and she has three of this guy's paintings and she says he's important. I think she's insane. It just looks like nothing to me. Like, I don't know. It just seems to me that for thirty-eight thousand dollars you could get something really nice.

CHARLES. Is that how much it is?

KATRINA. That one on the back wall? A hundred and twenty-five.

CHARLES. I've never even heard of this guy.

LYLE. I like them. I think they're brilliant, and vital.

KATRINA. You like them?

LYLE. I do. I really do.

> *(***MAE** *and* **RENE** *enter.* **RENE** *is a fashion plate.* **MAE** *wears a simple top with a pair of cargo pants and Birkenstocks.* **LYLE**'s *back is to them.)*

CHARLES. Don't turn around.

> *(***LYLE** *starts to turn around.)*

Don't turn around. Do NOT turn around.

> *(***RENE** *turns to* **MAE** *as soon as she sees* **LYLE**.*)*

RENE. He's here. Don't turn around don't turn around –

> *(But* **MAE** *has turned and seen them.)*

Why did you turn around? Now he's seen us. He'll think I'm stalking him. When I did not even know he'd be here.

MAE. He's Reg's cousin and Reg has been seeing Katrina, it makes sense that he would be here, Aunt Rene.

RENE. I can't see him.

MAE. That's ridiculous.

RENE. I am not ridiculous.

MAE. No, that's my point. You're not ridiculous. There was nothing said between you that compromised you. You are friends! You enjoyed his company.

RENE. He hasn't called.

MAE. Well, maybe you can just tell him, now that you see him here, that you'd love to have lunch sometime.

RENE. Lunch is pathetic.

MAE. Why is lunch pathetic?

RENE. *(Sneaking a look.)* He is so handsome.

    (To **MAE**.*)* Don't look. Don't look. Look at the paintings.

    (She looks at the paintings. **MAE** *follows orders and looks too.)*

Oh god. Another gallery opening. Everything looks the same. All those blotches, too much color, why are all the artists painting the same paintings all the time?

MAE. I don't know.

RENE. I wish you hadn't worn those sandals, darling. The rest of your outfit is charming, casual and charming, but the sandals.

MAE. They're really comfortable.

RENE. I'm just going to say it.

MAE. Don't – I don't really think –

RENE. *(Overlap.)* They make you look like a lesbian.

MAE. I like lesbians.

RENE. But you don't want to dress like them, sweetheart. A word to the wise.

LYLE. *(Calling to her.)* Rene!

    (KATRINA, REG, LYLE, *and* **CHARLES** *are approaching.)*

RENE. Look who's here.

LYLE. You look beautiful, Rene.

RENE. I'm so glad I've bumped into you, Lyle. You've been so elusive!

LYLE. Not elusive, no, not at all. I went down to the Pines for a few days.

RENE. Oh. I love it there.

LYLE. Really?

RENE. Darling. Those are my people.

LYLE. Mine too.

RENE. And the drive is so peaceful. You should have called! I would have loved to join you!

REG. Mae, what is up with the Birkenstocks? You finally coming out of the closet?

MAE. They're really comfortable.

(The WAITRESS *approaches.)*

WAITRESS. Excuse me. Is there a Mae Johnson here?

MAE. Yes, that's me.

WAITRESS. The valet attendant is having a problem with your car.

MAE. What's the problem?

WAITRESS. Something about the key?

MAE. I gave him the key.

WAITRESS. They're having some sort of problem.

KATRINA. Here's what you tell them. Put the key in the keyhole and turn.

MAE. It's a Prius.

KATRINA. Of course it is.

MAE. I'll just, I'll be right back.

(She goes. KATRINA *looks at* RENE.*)*

KATRINA. How can you let her drive one of those? They blow up, don't they?

REG. They accelerate.

KATRINA. They accelerate!

LYLE. That actually wasn't as big a problem as people said.

KATRINA. Maybe, but it was so great when it happened, wasn't it?

REG. People died!

KATRINA. Yes, I know, that's my point. They were all so smug about how many miles they get to the gallon, and then people DIED.

RENE. I've asked her repeatedly to use the Range Rover. Or the BMW. Both of them are much safer cars. I barely understand her anymore. You saw the sandals.

CHARLES. What do you think of the paintings, Rene?

RENE. Oh...

CHARLES. Lyle loves them.

RENE. *(A dazzling 180.)* They're magnificent!

 (They wander off.)

Scene Nine

(**MAE** *and the* **WAITRESS** *on the street.*)

WAITRESS. He'll be back in a minute.

(*They wait for a moment.*)

You know he really likes you.

MAE. The parking attendant?

WAITRESS. He kind of made me do this. I mean, I don't really like being used, who does? I just didn't have a lot of choice about it, 'cause I did this kind of dumb thing? A few times I did it. That's not really the point. The point is, he went to a lot of trouble. Not a lot of trouble. But even this much trouble, for a guy like that? He's pretty determined.

HENRY. (*Entering, behind.*) I can take it from here.

MAE. Not the parking attendant.

WAITRESS. No.

(*She ducks out.* **MAE** *shakes her head.*)

MAE. I told you. I don't want to talk to you.

HENRY. I'm not here to talk to you. I have to give something to you.

(*He holds out the spider brooch. She looks at it, startled.*)

MAE. Where did you get that?

HENRY. It's Rene's.

MAE. I know it's Rene's. Did you steal it?

HENRY. No. Steal? No!

MAE. Then how did you get it?

HENRY. I –

MAE. Don't tell me, I don't care. But she was looking for it.

HENRY. I'm sure she was.

MAE. Meaning what?

HENRY. Nothing, it's valuable.

MAE. I can't believe it.

HENRY. Are you okay?

MAE. She's just such a slut.

HENRY. No –

MAE. Don't defend her! She is! She was all, oh I have to show my little treasures to Lyle – who she's known for like a minute. And she didn't even remember that she GAVE it to you while you were – She didn't remember! Oh God. I'm so embarrassed.

HENRY. No. No no come –

MAE. It's just mortifying.

(She looks at the brooch, starts to sob a little.)

HENRY. Oh.

MAE. Sorry. Thank you. I'll just put it back with her things, she'll just pretend she misplaced it and it will all go away.

HENRY. That's what I was thinking.

*(**MAE** nods.)*

You look pretty. I like your sandals.

MAE. Oh. You're the only one. Everybody else thinks I look like a lesbian.

HENRY. Is that a bad thing?

MAE. Right? They're so much more comfortable, too. I feel a lot better. Like the earth is solid, under my feet. Those spikes, seriously, even when you get good at wearing them, you know that you could fall over and break your leg at any minute. And you know. You can't run in them.

HENRY. Where do you want to run to?

*(**MAE** looks at him, angry.)*

MAE. Haiti!

HENRY. Oh you're still doing that?

MAE. I know people think I'm kidding about that but I'm not!

HENRY. I don't think you're kidding, I just question your motives.

MAE. My motives are to help the poor.

HENRY. Wouldn't it make more sense just to kiss me?

(A beat.)

MAE. It would not.

HENRY. Are you sure?

MAE. I am quite sure. One thing has nothing to do with the other.

HENRY. Then you definitely should kiss me.

MAE. We clearly do not understand each other.

HENRY. I do understand that, Mae. I still think that you should kiss me.

MAE. I will not kiss you.

HENRY. This is not a binary situation! You said it yourself! You can still give the money away!

MAE. You had sex with my aunt.

HENRY. I like Rene. She's a fascinating woman.

MAE. And it's a great story, that you had the heiress, then you had the aunt. And then you had half of Long Island.

HENRY. Not half.

MAE. The figures shift daily I am sure.

HENRY. I am popular.

MAE. You will sleep with anything with a pulse!

HENRY. You knew that before! That's not what you're angry about.

MAE. I am not angry.

HENRY. Then you're not giving all your money away because you're mad at me.

MAE. In case it has escaped your attention, it is none of your business what I do with my money.

HENRY. Then you're only giving your money away in theory. I pissed you off, but not that much.

MAE. I spoke to a lawyer yesterday. I'm giving it all away.

> *(A beat.)*

HENRY. All of it.

MAE. Yes. So the money won't be there anymore. You don't have to go to all this trouble.

HENRY. I really think you should kiss me.

MAE. Do you think that will stop me from giving the money away?

HENRY. No one gives away all their money! They put it in foundations. Or, tax shelters.

MAE. No, I'm giving it away.

HENRY. Nobody does that.

MAE. It's historically rare, but it does happen. Francis of Assisi. The Buddha. Sting.

HENRY. He is not!

MAE. He is!

HENRY. You're giving all that money away.

MAE. Yes.

HENRY. What will you live on?

MAE. Hey moron, I'll get a job. People do. You know, people work. They know how to do things. I'll be one of them.

HENRY. Okay. Okay. However –

MAE. No. This isn't up for discussion. I'm giving my money away.

HENRY. So I really did piss you off.

MAE. This isn't about you.

HENRY. You know, altruism doesn't actually exist. They've proven this. It's all tied into the survival of the species.

MAE. They've proven that?

HENRY. Yes. Altruism in its essence is completely self-serving.

MAE. Where'd you hear that? On Facebook?

HENRY. Yes. You think if you give all that money away it will make you a good person, but the fact is, it is impossible to be a good person.

MAE. Are you still trying to convince me to kiss you?

HENRY. Is it working?

MAE. No, actually it's not.

HENRY. I'm not saying you're not a good person.

MAE. I'm not trying to be a good person. I'm just trying to be who I am. I have so much money, I don't exist.

HENRY. Most people think money makes them exist.

MAE. If they think that, then only the money exists. I would like to be a person who exists.

HENRY. Why can't you be a person who exists and also has money?

MAE. That's apparently not possible for me. All anyone ever sees is my money. I can't trust anybody.

HENRY. You trusted me.

MAE. And now I don't.

HENRY. You trusted me once, you can trust me again.

MAE. I trust you to completely lose interest in me, once I have no money.

HENRY. Then that is why you're doing it.

> (*A beat.*)

MAE. Leave me alone.

HENRY. Mae.

MAE. Leave me alone!

HENRY. I am not the enemy, Mae!

MAE. You are. You are! I'm not like you! Any of you. Love doesn't mean anything to you. I'm well aware that's why you slept with Rene, to make sure I could never trust you, because I did have feelings for you, Henry, I'm somebody who actually has feelings. And I know that makes me a freakshow. I understand that. Because feelings are contemptible now. They madden people.

CHARLES. No.

MAE. And I don't know why I came out like this. I was brought up the same way as everybody else out here, not exactly the same way because my mother like left my father and then she left me and all I have is all this money and this crazy aunt –

HENRY. Mae.

MAE. And I don't know why some people knew how to hang onto love and other people didn't. But I don't apologize for falling on this side of the fence.

HENRY. I don't want you to.

MAE. I've just been abandoned so many times. And you're somebody who abandons people. So I do just think, out of decency, you should leave me be. You stay with your side and I'll stay with my side and you know. Go to Haiti.

HENRY. What if I'm in love with you?

(A beat.)

MAE. Well that's unlikely isn't it?

HENRY. Unlikely yes, but apparently not impossible.

MAE. Look. I can't – I just – I can't have this. I honestly, I can't have you doing this.

HENRY. No, you're right, you're right.

*(****MAE**** turns to exit. Stops.)*

MAE. I don't want to go back in there. You broke my heart, and I hate you. But could you just hold me? Just for a second?

*(****HENRY**** nods. The hug turns into a kiss. The kiss is long, heartfelt, true. ****MAE**** tries to stop it but not very much. They cling to each other. Kiss again.)*

WAITRESS. Hello – excuse me. Hello?

*(****HENRY**** and ****MAE**** stop kissing, but just barely.)*

HENRY. Yes?

*(****MAE**** tries to step away from the embrace but he won't let her.)*

WAITRESS. I just, her aunt is looking for her.

> *(She thinks about saying more then decides
> not to. She turns abruptly and goes.)*

HENRY. *(Clinging to* **MAE.***)* Don't go.

MAE. I'll come back.

HENRY. No please no no no –

MAE. Henry. I'm not like you. If I say I'll come back, I'll come back.

> *(She kisses him. They can barely release each
> other. But she finally goes.)*

> *(***HENRY*** is alone. The sound of clapping in the
> dark.* **HENRY** *turns.* **CHARLES** *appears from the
> shadows.)*

CHARLES. That – was masterful.

HENRY. Charles.

CHARLES. I must say. It was a thrill, to watch.

HENRY. As always, happy to entertain.

CHARLES. That insight she had – that you slept with Rene to punish her, because she had the appalling impulse to fall in love with you! I hadn't even thought of that.

HENRY. No?

CHARLES. These women are smarter than they look.

> *(A beat.)*

HENRY. You know what? I'm not talking to you about Mae. I'm not doing it.

CHARLES. You're never going to get your hands on that money.

HENRY. It's not about –

CHARLES. *(Overlap.)* It's completely about the money, you wouldn't even look at her, if she didn't have all that money.

HENRY. I mean it. Not another word. We've been friends a long time.

CHARLES. Is that what we are?

> *(A beat.)*

HENRY. Charles. I got drunk one night a couple years ago, and I let you suck me off. That's all it was. It wasn't anything else.

CHARLES. I was there too.

HENRY. I was drunk, Charles! When I'm drunk I'll pretty much let anyone suck me off. And let me tell you something else, I am not the only guy in history who has taken this position.

CHARLES. Yes, there's a long line of men who have taken that position.

HENRY. Think whatever you want to think, I don't care.

CHARLES. You'll never be faithful to her.

HENRY. What do you care?

CHARLES. She's a nice person.

HENRY. You hate nice people!

CHARLES. So do you!

HENRY. I like her.

CHARLES. There's a deathless declaration.

HENRY. Okay. I love her.

CHARLES. You LOVE her. Did you see what she was wearing tonight? She looks like a lesbian!

HENRY. Love is strange, Charles. It doesn't do what you think it's going to do. And you know what else? I like women. I like the way they smell. I like the things they laugh at. I like having sex with women. I love it! And I love Mae. And honestly, I don't know why you find that so offensive. I don't know why you need me to be gay. What would happen if you could force me, somehow, to be something I'm not? Would it make you feel better? I wish you felt better, Charles. Because maybe then you would just leave me alone.

(He shrugs and goes, leaving **CHARLES** *alone.)*

Scene Ten

(**RENE** *in bed, laughing. She is having a great time with a very athletic lover. The sheets cover him for a moment.*)

RENE. Don't stop don't stop, oh god oh god! OH GOD.

(*Her lover is revealed. It's* **REG.** *He is breathless.*)

REG. You are fantastic.

RENE. Me? I'm just lying here!

REG. You're lying there with such incredible, wow.

RENE. You're sweet.

REG. I'm not sweet. I'm happy! You're fucking awesome, Rene. That was. Holy shit. You are really fun to have sex with. Man.

(**RENE** *laughs at him.*)

No kidding, I haven't had that much fun in I don't know how long. Oh, boy. You're fucking awesome Rene. Wow. You're so fucking warm, and soft –

RENE. Oh, soft. Darling. That's code for fat.

REG. You're not fat! You're gorgeous. Are you kidding?

RENE. A momentary insecurity.

REG. I hate that. A woman like you is insecure? Over what? Don't tell me. I know what. The yin yang of this country is totally fucked. Women are horrible, men are assholes and then there's you lying there thinking you're fat. It's so fucking stupid, really. You're so beautiful. I could look at you forever.

RENE. You know, Reg – you are really lovely.

REG. Thanks.

(*They kiss. He gets out of bed.*)

But could we really not tell anyone about this?

RENE. (*Abashed.*) Oh –

REG. 'Cause I would like it just to be – whatever it is. I just mean, we could go out to dinner, or we could go to a party or something, and nobody else has to know that we're like totally hot for each other. Because you know they'll have something to say about it. And they won't be particularly nice.

RENE. *(Thinking.)* A secret romance. Played out in public. It's – devastating.

REG. Right?

RENE. What about Lyle?

REG. What about him?

RENE. He's your cousin, darling.

REG. Only sort of.

RENE. But honestly – honestly, is this fair to him? I think he may have feelings for me.

REG. Oh shit. No no no. He's gay. He's like, GAY.

RENE. He is?

REG. Well, sure. Don't get me wrong, he's a totally nice guy.

RENE. Are you gay?

REG. No! What? No.

RENE. I just don't quite understand what is going on.

REG. Oh nothing, really. It was just Henry.

RENE. Henry? What does he have to do with this?

REG. Well, that's why Lyle started being so nice to you. Henry asked him to kind of distract you, so that he could have a little time alone with Mae, to you know. Work things out.

RENE. Henry – asked him – what did he ask him?

REG. Oh. No. Come on. Don't be mad. Who cares? I mean seriously. They're working things out and we're having a good time. What's wrong with that?

RENE. Nothing.

REG. Good.

> *(He kisses her and goes.)*

> *(Over his shoulder.)* You want to have dinner tomorrow?

RENE. That sounds divine. Simply terrific.

> *(But she is pissed.)*

Scene Eleven

(**HENRY** *at an outdoor restaurant.* **RENE** *approaches.)*

RENE. Henry.

HENRY. Rene. You look stunning, as usual.

RENE. Flatterer.

(The **WAITRESS** *approaches with blue martinis.)*

HENRY. I took the liberty of ordering for you.

RENE. And of course you know my drink.

HENRY. How could I forget? The color is brilliant, and it matches your eyes.

RENE. You're a terrible flirt and a terrible man.

HENRY. Come on, Rene. We had a good time, didn't we? I have no regrets.

RENE. Nor I, no no no.

HENRY. Good.

RENE. I heard you and Mae have come to an understanding.

HENRY. I'd prefer not to talk about Mae.

RENE. Really?

HENRY. Really. I'd like to keep what's between us private.

RENE. When there's six hundred million dollars on the table? Good luck.

HENRY. I'm not after Mae's money.

RENE. I'm relieved to hear it. I love her very much. I wouldn't want anyone toying with her affections when they were secretly concerned about other things.

HENRY. My interest in her affection is sincere.

RENE. Of course no one wants to believe that more than me. But how could I help but be confused, when your feelings for me seemed equally sincere. I would hate to think that you weren't a sincere person.

HENRY. I am a sincere person.

RENE. And your friend Lyle, he's sincere as well? Such a nice man. He seems very sincere. His attentions to me, have certainly seemed sincere. And I'm told that was your idea. For Lyle to come calling on me. In spite of the fact that he's gay as a post.

HENRY. My –

RENE. I found out about your little deal, Henry. Very amusing. Knowing how heartbroken I was, because you yourself had treated me so cruelly. All I was looking for was a little love. And you sent your friend Lyle, gay gay gay, to trick me. Make fun of me. Carelessly humiliate me once again.

HENRY. That's not –

RENE. If you even try to deny it, I'll tell Mae all about it!

HENRY. She is – not – going to care about that.

RENE. The manipulating, the game playing, the meanness of spirit. She'll care. She loves me.

HENRY. Rene. I do love her.

RENE. How much? Enough to give her up?

(A beat.)

Not as much as that?

It's fine, Henry. It's just that Mae is so idealistic and I know she's been worried about your character. It would be awful if someone were to shatter the delicate balance that you two seem to have established. But that's not going to happen. I am so thrilled that she's getting married.

HENRY. Marriage!

RENE. You don't love her that much?

HENRY. There's a lot of room between love and marriage.

RENE. There didn't use to be.

HENRY. Yeah, but –

RENE. But you love her and you're sincere, and she's worth six hundred million dollars, Henry, while you're poor as a church mouse, what's the problem? I never married myself and I always wanted to. I want her wedding to be perfect. It's not going to be easy because she has such peculiar views. But I know you and I can keep her steered right. She's an heiress. We both need to make sure she doesn't forget what that means.

HENRY. Hang on. You want me to –

RENE. I don't think I'm saying anything so terribly radical! What's that old saying, keep your friends close and your enemies closer? That's all I'm talking about.

(**HENRY** *thinks about this.*)

HENRY. How are your finances, Rene?

RENE. Well if you must know, they are not all one could wish.

HENRY. Are they not.

RENE. A woman alone, often saddled with a child I was not entirely suited to raise? There were some issues.

HENRY. Nothing you couldn't handle by the looks of it.

RENE. My entire life is wrapped up in that girl.

HENRY. And her trust.

RENE. Yes she does trust me.

HENRY. That's not what I meant.

RENE. Isn't it funny how many meanings that word has!

HENRY. Yes, it is. So let's make a few assumptions about the word "trust" in this situation. You are the primary trustee?

RENE. And thank goodness for that; her mother is completely unreliable. Mae is getting a bit flighty herself, lately. All of this talk about "giving" so much of that fortune away. I was contacted by a lawyer just the other day. He wants to look at all the documents, files, records, receipts! Who can ever keep track of receipts, I'd like to meet that person.

HENRY. So he hasn't yet actually looked through the documents and records and receipts.

RENE. It takes a little while to get all those papers organized. There have been a few difficulties.

HENRY. Is the money all there?

(**RENE** *laughs at that.*)

RENE. Why do you want to know? Would it change your feelings about her? All that love. Does it change, if there's less money? You don't love her that much? I would hate for her to hear that that was why you wouldn't marry her.

HENRY. I never said –

RENE. Good. I love a good wedding.

HENRY. How much of the money is gone?

RENE. You know, Henry, a lot of details really might just spoil the mood. There's plenty to go around, provided Mae doesn't do anything stupid. You tell me your affections are sincere. I have every reason to believe you. In spite of the manipulation, and the infidelity, and all the cruel, cruel frat boy humor, often exercised at my expense. I trust you!

HENRY. So you want me to marry her. And help you. When these difficulties show their face.

RENE. We can help each other. Or not.

(She smiles at **HENRY***. Puts her hand on his.)*

Good! We're on the same page. Let's stay there.

(The **WAITRESS** *appears with a tray of drinks.)*

Scene Twelve

(*The* **WAITRESS** *turns to serve drinks to* **HENRY**, *who has just entered.*)

WAITRESS. This is a crisp chardonnay with light oak from a boutique vineyard from the coastal region just south of Ojai, that's California, and a merlot-cab blend from Argentina. And sparkling water.

HENRY. Thanks.

(*He takes a glass.*)

(**RENE** *and* **REG** *enter above and flirt, unseen by* **HENRY** *and the* **WAITRESS**.)

WAITRESS. I heard you're getting married!

HENRY. Engaged.

WAITRESS. Oh, uh-huh. I just didn't think that was your thing. Course, she's got all that money. That's a lot of zeroes.

HENRY. Thank you.

WAITRESS. Is there a prenup? 'Cause when one person has all the money and the other person doesn't that's usually what they do.

HENRY. You know, I love her and I'm really happy.

WAITRESS. Oh, I know.

(*She winks at* **HENRY**.)

(**RENE** *pushes* **REG** *away and turns her attention to* **HENRY**. *She is wearing a spectacular outfit.*)

RENE. Henry!

HENRY. Rene. You look wonderful as always.

RENE. Thank you, darling. It's such a special occasion for all of us. Mae will be down in a minute.

WAITRESS. This is a crisp chardonnay with light oak –

RENE. I know what it is. It's my house. Katrina! Charles. Hello, Lyle.

(The others are entering. They exchange kisses.)

CHARLES. You look glorious, Rene. And so does your lawn.

RENE. I know you disapprove Charles but I don't care. I didn't invent it and I'm not the only one who does it either and it looks pretty! And I'm giving people jobs too!

LYLE. Ignore him, Rene, he's just being contrary.

RENE. As always.

KATRINA. Henry! Congratulations. Who would have thought.

HENRY. Indeed.

KATRINA. People are placing bets up and down the coast. How long it's going to take you to cheat on her.

HENRY. Is that a joke or an offer, Katrina?

KATRINA. Which would be my point. Where's the lucky girl?

RENE. *(Entering.)* She's coming! She'll be down in a minute.

KATRINA. *(To* **REG**, *suspicious.)* What are you doing here?

REG. I was invited.

KATRINA. What were you doing upstairs?

REG. Brushing my hair.

> **(MAE** *comes in behind. She is wearing a beautiful dress and a strappy pair of high-heeled sandals.)*

RENE. There's our princess!

> *(She starts applauding. The others do as well.)*

MAE. Stop it. Oh come on stop it.

RENE. The bride-to-be.

MAE. Yes. Yes!

RENE. You look gorgeous! Doesn't she look gorgeous?

CHARLES. Wonderful.

LYLE. Congratulations, Mae.

KATRINA. That dress is divine.

MAE. Aunt Rene, I couldn't find my bracelet, I left it right on my dresser and now it's gone. My mom sent it, from Japan.

(Behind her, the **WAITRESS** *looks up.)*

HENRY. We'll find it.

WAITRESS. Here it is!

(She pulls it out of her pocket.)

It was in the kitchen. I was just going to bring it up to you.

MAE. Oh, thank you.

HENRY. Yes, thank you.

WAITRESS. I'll go get more wine.

(She goes. **MAE** *pulls* **HENRY** *into a corner.)*

MAE. I can't breathe. Rene bought me this dress and it's really tight.

HENRY. You look pretty hot in it.

MAE. The shoes are killing me. They're the only ones that go with the dress. I don't really care what goes with the dress, but Rene is, this is a big deal to her. I had to get my picture taken all afternoon. They want me to register online for wedding presents. Crystal bowls! Champagne flutes! My head hurts. And I'm not kidding this dress is so tight. I can't breathe.

HENRY. Maybe we should get out of here.

MAE. Wouldn't that be rude?

HENRY. Who cares? We need to go to Haiti now, right now. We can get married at the airport. It'll be a story, we can tell our kids.

MAE. I – would love that.

HENRY. You would?

MAE. But this wedding is so important to Rene.

HENRY. Listen. Listen, Mae. There's something you need to know. About all of this.

RENE. A toast, a toast!

*(***MAE** *turns toward* **RENE.***)*

HENRY. Wait.

MAE. There's a toast.

HENRY. Can't we just go? I love you. Let's go!

RENE. There seems to be some discord, between our bride- and groom-to-be! Groom, we all hope you haven't disappointed her already!

HENRY. If we have a problem? It will be that I love her too much!

(**MAE** *looks at him, startled, takes a step back.*)

MAE. What does that mean?

RENE. Oo, the bride didn't like that!

MAE. I just don't know what it means.

RENE. And you will never know!

(*She laughs, a shred diabolical. The others laugh.*)

Of all the things we don't know, that is the worst one. Which is why marriage is such a serious business. It's not for the faint of heart! But what is, in this world? The easy things are so often not worth having. Wealth, jewelry, beautiful clothes, a trip to Paris, a weekend on a yacht – okay I'm just kidding, those things are worth having!

(*They all laugh.*)

But it's the hard things – tenderness, faithfulness, devotion – that cost, but reward us too. So many people don't even try to love anymore. And that is the tragedy of our time. For love – true love – is the only thing worth having. It is the blessing we all yearn for. The hope of our youth. The benediction of our old age. The promise of life. To love.

ALL. To love!

(*They hold up their glasses.*)

(*Blackout.*)

End of Play